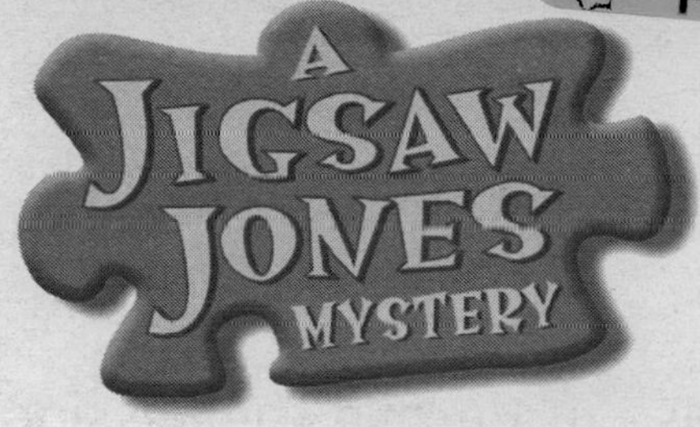

The Case of the Christmas Snowman

The Jigsaw Jones Mysteries

#1 The Case of Hermie the Missing Hamster

#2 The Case of the Christmas Snowman

Coming Soon

#3 The Case of the Secret Valentine

The Case of the Christmas Snowman

by James Preller
illustrated by R.W.Alley

A
LITTLE APPLE
PAPERBACK

SCHOLASTIC INC.
New York Toronto London Auckland Sydney
Mexico City New Delhi Hong Kong

For

Nicholas

Book design by Dawn Adelman

ISBN 0-590-69126-0

22 21 20 19 18 17 16 2 3/0

Printed in the U.S.A. 40

First Scholastic printing, November 1998

Contents

Chapter One

A Missing Coin

I glanced at the clock. It read 3:51. Two minutes had passed since the last time I looked. Lucy Hiller was now twenty-one minutes late. Some days time flies. Other days it crawls by like a sick cockroach. Today was one of those days. Yeesh.

I was in my winter office, in a corner of my basement. My regular office, a tree house in the backyard, was shut down for the season. Too much ice and snow. Fortunately, my parents let me set up shop down here. It wasn't heaven, but I suppose

it was all right. I had my own desk. On the wall behind the desk a sign read, JIGSAW JONES, PRIVATE EYE. I made it myself.

I sipped on my second glass of grape juice. And waited.

It was now exactly 3:52.

In the Jones house, you don't need a doorbell. Our dog, a big Newfoundland named Rags, tells when someone is at the door. When he barked, I knew that Lucy Hiller had arrived.

"Theodore — er, I mean Jigsaw — your visitor is here," my mom called.

A soft voice said, "Thank you, Mrs. Jones." I watched as a pair of bright red boots came down the stairs. The boots were attached to Lucy Hiller.

Lucy sat in a chair across from my desk. Her hair was curly and black. Her eyes were round and brown.

"Grape juice?" I offered.

Lucy politely shook her head. "No,

JIGSAW JONES, PRIVATE EYE
$1.00 in advance

thanks." She showed me her straight white teeth. Then her smile disappeared. "I've been told that you are the best detective in second grade."

I didn't disagree.

Lucy chewed her lip. "I've got a problem," she said.

"I make problems go away," I said. "But it will cost you. I get a dollar a day."

Lucy placed some money on the desk. My jaw dropped. It showed a picture of Abraham Lincoln. "That's a five-dollar bill," I said.

"If you can get me out of this mess," Lucy said, "it will be worth it."

I opened my detective journal to a clean page. I missed my partner, Mila. But she had a music lesson. I'd have to start without her. "I'm all ears," I said.

Lucy talked fast. "Okay. Last Friday I borrowed a coin from my father's coin collection. It was an Indian-head nickel and

it was very valuable. I wanted to bring it to school and show everybody."

"Let me guess," I interrupted. "It's missing."

Lucy nodded unhappily. I started to hand her a box of Kleenex. But her eyes were clear. Lucy Hiller wasn't the crying type. She continued, "Okay. So I showed the coin to Bigs Maloney during recess. He was building that snowman of his, the huge one by the basketball courts. Well, Bigs really loved it. He thought the coin was the coolest thing. So I let him hold it for the rest of the day." Lucy paused. "Now Bigs says he can't find it."

I was stunned. "Why — of *all* people — did you give the coin to Bigs Maloney?"

Lucy's cheeks flushed red. "I don't know," she said, looking down.

I thought for a moment. A question hung in the air. I finally asked it. "Do you think Bigs is telling the truth?"

Lucy lifted her head and looked at me. Now her eyes seemed glassy and wet. Lucy Hiller would need that Kleenex after all.

After she left, I took out my markers. I wrote in my detective journal **SUSPECTS**. I underlined it in purple. Then I wrote the name **Bigs Maloney**.

And I knew this case meant trouble.

"Bigs" trouble.

Chapter Two

A Message to Mila

I wrote a message to Mila. It was in code. Rags watched as I worked. I wasn't worried. Rags couldn't read. To be honest, Rags couldn't do much — except eat and sleep and bark and drool. Then he drooled some more. Like my dad says, Rags may be a mess. But he is *our* mess. So we loved him anyway.

When you're a detective, you've got to know about secret codes. It's part of the job. I have a book called *Detective Tricks*

You Can Do. That's how Mila and I learned mirror writing.

First I got two sheets of paper. Then I wrote the message on one sheet. Now came the tricky part. I turned the page over and taped another sheet on top. I held the paper up to a window, copying the message backward. Next, I removed the first sheet — and I had a mirror message.

To read it, just hold the paper up to a mirror. My message looked like this:

MILA. BIG CASE. SEE YOU ON THE BUS.
DESTROY THIS MESSAGE!
— JIGSAW

"Dinner's almost ready!" my dad called.

"Now?" I asked. "But I've got to drop off a message to Mila."

My dad sighed, glancing at his watch. "Okay, pal. Lickety-split. Just run down the block and back — and make it quick."

Mila was not only my partner but my best friend. She worked with me on all the big cases. I paid her fifty cents a day.

Getting dressed to go outside in the snow took longer than going to Mila's house. That's the big problem with winter. You spend half the day putting on boots, scarves, and mittens. Then you spend the other half taking them off again. I guess it beats freezing like a human Popsicle. Anyway, I handed the message to Mila and was back in time to complain about the meat loaf.

There are five kids in my family — four boys and one girl. I'm the youngest. Then there are my parents and Grams. Grams moved in with us a couple of years ago. My folks said she was too old to be on her own. That was fine by me. She always gave me butterscotch.

Dinnertime was always pretty crazy. Everybody jabbering away or rushing off

somewhere in a big hurry. My dad says you can get more peace and quiet in a bowling alley. But he didn't really mind. Sometimes he'd just smile and listen to us chatter away. He called it a joyful racket.

Whatever that means.

I usually do my homework after dinner. My teacher, Ms. Gleason, started this thing called Read-A-Mania. If you read for fifteen minutes a day, you get a sticker. After you earn one hundred stickers, then Ms.

Gleason treats you to ice cream. I have fifty-three stickers already. I told Ms. Gleason that chocolate ice cream was my favorite.

After homework, I sometimes watch television. Or do a jigsaw puzzle. Or bug my sister. Or spy on my brothers. But tonight I needed to think about the case.

Too bad the dishes came first.

Chapter Three

The Christmas Snowman

The next morning I met Mila at the bus stop. She was lucky. The stop was right in front of her house.

When Mila came out, she was singing "The Muffin Man." Well, not exactly. It *sounded* like "The Muffin Man," but the words were different. Ms. Gleason taught it to us in school last week. Ms. Gleason was always changing the words to songs. Mila sang:

"Oh, have you seen my big snowman,
My big snowman, my big snowman,
Oh, have you seen my big snowman,
Who melts in my front yard?"

We sat in the back of the bus together. Mila slid her finger across her nose. It was our secret signal. It meant that she had read the message.

"So what's the big case?" Mila asked.

I told her about Lucy's visit . . . the missing Indian-head nickel . . . and Bigs Maloney.

Mila crossed her arms. She rocked back and forth. Mila finally said, "Let's have a talk with Bigs Maloney." I didn't say a word. But I knew Mila was right. We had to talk to Bigs. There was no way around it. The idea didn't have me doing cartwheels. See, the last time I saw Bigs Maloney, he hit me with a snowball. Right in the back.

Trouble followed Bigs Maloney like a shadow. Just last week Bigs let the hamsters loose in class. He told Ms. Gleason it was an accident. But I think it was on purpose. Once, during Halloween, Bigs poured ketchup all over his shirt. He pretended it was blood. He made gross sounds and fell on the cafeteria floor. That was Bigs Maloney for you.

The bus came to a stop. Mila pointed across the school yard. "There he is, our number-one suspect," she said. Bigs was alone, making a snowman. Mila and I trudged through the snow. Bigs Maloney was the roughest, toughest kid in class. His real name was Charlie. But everyone called him Bigs because he was so big. I noticed the snaps were wrong on his new-looking winter coat.

"If it isn't the great detective, Jigsaw Jones," Bigs said. "How's the back?" He slapped fistfuls of snow into the snowman.

"It's been better," I said.

Bigs suddenly looked worried. "You're not going to tell, are you?" he asked.

"I'm not a tattler," I said.

"It was an accident," Bigs claimed.

"Some accident," I said. "You screamed, 'Bull's-eye!' "

"Look, Jigsaw," he said. "I didn't mean anything. It's just that when it snows, I *have* to make snowballs. And if I make a snowball, then I *have* to throw it. It's not my fault you made a perfect target."

Oh, brother.

Mila nodded toward the snowman. "What are you up to, Bigs?"

Bigs smiled wide. He pointed proudly. "Isn't this the greatest snowman you've ever seen?"

"It's big," Mila said.

Bigs made a face. "You ain't seen nothing yet," he said. "I've been building this guy for three days. It's going to be my best snowman ever."

"Listen, Bigs," Mila said. "We came to ask you a few questions."

"Yeah, what about?"

"About Lucy Hiller," Mila said. "And about a missing Indian-head nickel."

Bigs looked down. He crushed a snowball with his foot. "I lost it," he said. "It was an accident."

"An accident," I repeated. "I've heard that before."

Big mistake.

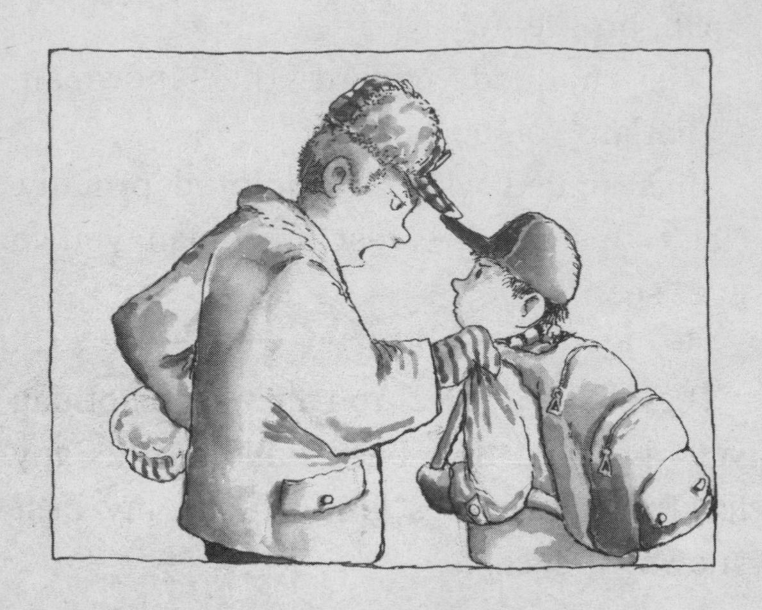

Bigs scowled. He put a hand on my shoulder. It felt like a bear's claw. "Just what does that mean? Do you think I'm a liar?"

I stood nose to nose with Bigs Maloney. Actually, it was nose to neck. But I didn't back down. "Look, Bigs," I said. "I don't *think* anything. I'm a detective. I ask questions."

Bbbbbring!

"It's the school bell," Mila said. "We'd better get inside."

Chapter Four

Planning a Party

Room 201 was as busy as a beehive. Everyone was buzzing about the class party on Friday. We were going to have a grab bag — and a talent show. A lot of kids were filling up the gift box with their grab bag presents. On Friday we'd all take turns reaching into the box. Ms. Gleason told us that the present could be any book we wanted. But it *had* to be a book. That was fine with me. I loved books. Most of them, anyway.

Ms. Gleason was tall with short hair.

Some kids said it was blonde. Other kids said it was red. I thought her hair looked like the color of maple leaves in October. Anyway, Ms. Gleason was the nicest teacher in the school. And she was very pretty.

For the class party, everybody had special jobs. I had to bring in napkins. I asked my mom to get cool ones, like Spider-Man or Star Wars napkins. Ms. Gleason told us she was ordering pizza for the whole class. Everybody cheered, except for Ralphie Jordan. The poor guy was allergic to cheese.

We were too excited to do much work. Ms. Gleason told us that we were off-the-wall. She said, “With vacation almost here, I know it’s hard to get work done. We’ll take it easy this week.”

Ms. Gleason gave us an extra recess. In the playground, everybody wanted to talk about the talent show. Mila said that she

was going to sing. Joey Pignattano was going to do a Tae Kwon Do demonstration. Danika Starling and Kim Lewis were teaming up for a puppet show. Even Bigs Maloney said he had a wonderful surprise planned.

I didn't say much. Why bother? Everyone had a special talent except me. I couldn't think of anything.

In the afternoon we gave our holiday reports. Ms. Gleason said that four kids could give their reports each day. She said, "I'm very excited to hear your reports, boys and girls. I can't wait to learn about the different ways we all celebrate holiday traditions. This way we can understand and appreciate one another better."

We were allowed to pick any holiday that our family celebrated during the winter. That day two kids talked about Christmas and the baby Jesus. Then it was Geetha Nair's turn. Her parents were from India. At the beginning of winter, Geetha's family celebrated *Diwali.* It was also called the Festival of Lights. It sounded okay, except there was too much cleaning.

Geetha also brought in a clay lamp called a *dipa* lamp. I drew a quick picture in my journal. It looked like this:

Then it was Mila's turn. I paid extra-special attention. "Last year we started a new tradition in my family," Mila said. "We go to a store and buy a new toy, but we can't open it. Then we go to the Salvation Army and put it in a box with other toys. The toys go to needy children."

Mila looked at Ms. Gleason. "That's about it," Mila said.

"Thank you, Mila," Ms. Gleason said.

"That was very nice. How does it make you feel to give away a brand-new toy?"

Mila said, "It's kind of hard. But I guess I like it. Alice, that's my stepmom, says it's important to help others — especially during the holidays. I think she's right."

Ms. Gleason put an arm around Mila. She thanked everybody for their reports. And she thanked the rest of us for being such good listeners.

Then we worked on our math worksheets.

I liked mine, because it turned math into a mystery. It was called "Janitor Math."

Here's what it said:

Mr. Walker, the school janitor, has a big job planned. He has to paint room numbers on the classroom doors. His favorite numbers are 1, 2, and 3. Write the six different room numbers he can make by changing the place values of 1, 2, and 3.

That part was easy. I wrote my answers fast, with only a few cross-outs. My numbers were:

123 231 312
~~23~~
213 321 132
~~123~~

Then we had to answer a question. *What is Mr. Walker's favorite room number?*____ There were two clues. It was like solving a puzzle:

Clue #1: The largest digit is in the tens place. 3

Clue #2: The smallest digit is in the hundreds place. 1

I wrote my answer quickly 132.

I wished math could always be so interesting. It made me feel like a detective. Besides, it made me think about our own school janitor, Mr. Copabianco. I liked him because he was so friendly. We all called him "Good Old Mr. Copabianco." He seemed to like it.

I noticed that Mila spent a lot of time talking to Lucy Hiller. Lucy still looked sad about that missing coin. Then I suddenly had an idea. It was so easy. There was a coin store right in town. I'd just buy Lucy a new one.

After all, how much could it cost to buy a lousy nickel?

Chapter Five

Uncle Sam's Coin Shop

My brother Billy pulled over to the curb in front of Uncle Sam's Coin Shop. Billy was sixteen. He always gave me rides. Mostly because he liked driving my mom's car.

"Are you coming in?" I asked.

"Nah," he answered. "I'll just cruise around. How long you gonna be?"

"About twenty minutes," I said.

"You got it, Jigsaw." He pulled away fast.

Bells jingled when I opened the store door. A man sitting behind a glass counter looked up from a thick book. He nodded and went back to reading. A half-eaten sandwich lay by his elbow. I figured that he must be Uncle Sam himself.

The light was dim. Glass shelves were everywhere. Piles of boxes were on the floor. The place had a funny smell, like onions. Uncle Sam's Coin Shop didn't look like much of a store. It seemed more like a messy garage.

"Anything I can do for you, lad?" Uncle Sam asked.

"I want to buy a nickel," I said.

Uncle Sam jerked a thumb toward the corner. "Most nickels are in one of those boxes over there. You'll have to hunt around." His eyes returned to the book.

I didn't move. "Actually," I admitted, "I was wondering if you could help me."

Uncle Sam folded down the corner of a page, took a big bite of his sandwich, and closed the book. He wiped his mouth with the back of his sleeve. "I don't remember

DIMES
1925
-1937
PENNIES

seeing you before," he said. "Is this your first time here?"

I nodded.

"Well, you've come to the right place," Uncle Sam said. "How long have you been a numismatist?"

"A numi-what?" I said.

Uncle Sam flashed a grin. He had a gold tooth. "A numismatist," he said. "It's a big, fancy word that means coin collector."

"I'm not a numa-, a numis-, a coin collector," I said. "I'm a detective. My name is Jigsaw. I'm working on a case."

Uncle Sam reached out and shook my hand. "Pleased to meet you, Jigsaw," he said. "How can I help you?"

I told him that I was looking for a 1937D Indian-head nickel. "It's very rare," I added.

"Rare?" Uncle Sam said. "I don't think so. I'm sure I've got a few around here someplace." He reached for a small red book. It was called *A Guidebook of United*

State Coins. "Let's just check and see," he said. "Do you want just the price? Or would you like to walk out that door a little smarter than when you walked in?"

I hesitated. "A little smarter, I guess."

"Good lad," Uncle Sam said. "There are different kinds of coin collectors. Most youngsters start with what's called a 'series' collection. That means you pick one kind of coin — say a Lincoln penny — and try to collect one from every date it

was struck. Nineteen sixty, nineteen sixty-one, nineteen sixty-two, and so on."

He continued, "Another way of collecting is called 'kind.' That's when you don't care about dates. Instead, for example, you might try to collect every kind of nickel that's been made. There are Liberty-head nickels, Indian heads, Jefferson heads, and so on and so forth."

I scratched my head.

"Do you understand?" he asked.

"Sort of," I answered.

Uncle Sam ran a finger down the book. Now, to buy the nickel you asked about — a 1937D — will cost you anywhere between seventy-five cents and two dollars."

"Wow," I said. "Two dollars for one nickel." I suddenly remembered there was something else about Lucy's nickel. I checked my detective journal. "Oh, yeah," I said. "It has a three-legged buffalo on the back."

"Ah, now we're talking," Uncle Sam said. "The three-legged buffalo, 1937D, is quite special. Let me show you." He picked up a set of keys and walked around the counter. He opened a glass case and handed me a coin. "See that?" he said. "Three legs."

Sure enough, the buffalo on the back of the coin was missing a leg. "But why did they make it with only three legs?" I asked.

"It was an error, a mistake," Uncle Sam said. "It happens sometimes. Coins with

errors are worth a lot more." He checked the book again. "A three-legged buffalo, 1937D nickel sells for anywhere from two hundred to five hundred dollars. Depending on the condition."

I gulped.

The bells above the door jingled again. "Hello, Ernie," Uncle Sam greeted the new customer.

I heard a loud honk outside the door. It was either my brother Billy or an angry goose. "I have to go," I told Uncle Sam. "Thank you, sir."

"Come back anytime, detective," Uncle Sam called out. He gave me a wink. The gold tooth glittered in his mouth.

Chapter Six

Words in a Sentence

"Five hundred dollars?!" Mila exclaimed. "For a nickel?"

We were supposed to be doing our homework in my basement. But we were really going over the facts of the case. See, mysteries are like jigsaw puzzles. First you have to lay out the pieces. Then you try to figure it out.

"I still can't believe that Lucy's father let her have such a valuable coin," I said.

Mila shook her head. "He doesn't know yet. Lucy borrowed it without asking." I

JIGSAW JONES,
PRIVATE EYE

took out my markers and drew a picture of Lucy. I tried to make Lucy look really worried. But instead, it turned out looking like she was going to throw up. But that's okay. People are hard to draw.

My mom came down with a snack. Two Christmas cookies. They were still warm. "How's the homework coming along?" she asked.

"Uh, fine, Mom," I said, crossing my fingers. Mila didn't say anything. I think that's what gave us away.

"Okay, you two," my mom said. "Mystery time is over. Get to work." She left us alone, shaking her head as she climbed the stairs.

On Tuesday nights we had to use ten

spelling words in sentences, plus a bonus word. The words we had to use were:

sweep	*shoe*
shut	*find*
finish	*large*
room	*keep*
thing	*teeth*

I could choose between four bonus words. They were: *Santa Claus, presents, dreidel,* and *candles.* I wrote my sentences

slowly. Ms. Gleason says we have to be careful with our spelling and punctuation.

Mila looked at my work. She said that I made some mistakes.

"Who are our suspects?" Mila asked.

I didn't even need to look in my journal. "There's just one," I said. "Bigs Maloney."

"Any clues?" she asked.

"None," I said.

Mila and I sat in unhappy silence. She rocked back and forth, singing quietly:

"Oh, have you seen my lost nickel,
My lost nickel, my lost nickel,
Oh, have you seen my lost nickel?
Bigs Maloney had it last!"

It wasn't one of her better songs — and I told her so. Finally I stood up. "There's only one thing to do," I said. "Tomorrow we've got to search Bigs Maloney's room.

He might have kept the coin and hidden it."

"I don't know, Jigsaw," Mila said. "How are we going to do that?"

"I'll think of something," I answered.

Mila frowned. "That's what scares me."

Chapter Seven

The Secret Deadly Mission

Mila and I went to Bigs Maloney's house after school on Wednesday. Standing outside his door, Mila took a deep breath. We were both nervous. "Remember the plan," I said.

I leaned on the bell.

Bigs opened the door. "Hi, Bigs," we said. He was surprised to see us. Bigs stood there looking at us.

"Er, can we come in for a minute?" Mila said.

"MOM!" Bigs screamed. "Is it okay if I have friends inside?"

Mrs. Maloney called back, "Friends? That's fine, Charlie. But no wet boots on the rug."

"My mom's busy with the twins," Bigs explained. "She's *always* busy with the twins." We took our boots off and placed them on a mat. My big toe was cold. I had a hole in my sock.

"Can we go in your room?" I said.

"Yeah, I guess." Bigs led us into a small bedroom. Dinosaur posters were on the walls. Toy dinosaurs were on the floor. There was a toy box so jammed with stuff, the lid couldn't close.

Bigs sat on his bed. "So?" he said.

"I wanted to say I was sorry," I said. I crossed my fingers behind my back. I wasn't really sorry, but I had to say something. "You've got me wrong, Bigs. I never said you were a liar."

Bigs shrugged and waited.

"We were just asking," I explained.

"I'm not dumb," Bigs said. "I know you think I stole it. But I didn't."

We stared at each other. The silence lasted a few seconds. It felt like hours. Mila finally said, "Hey, Bigs, I didn't know your mom had twins. Could I meet them?"

Bigs brightened. "Sure," he said. "They're eating now. It's pretty funny to watch them throw stuff on the floor." At the door Bigs turned. "Aren't you coming, Jigsaw?"

"Can I wait here?" I asked. "I want to look at your dinosaurs."

Bigs shrugged and left the room with Mila.

I was alone.

First I looked through his sock drawer. That's where kids keep a lot of their best stuff. Nothing there. I felt under his mattress. The only thing I found was a toy Pachycephalosaurus and half a bag of stale

popcorn. Then I checked the closet. I looked through the pockets of his new coat. They were filled with junk — plastic toys and stuff — but no coin. Next to that, I noticed Bigs still had his old coat. The one he used to wear every day. It was green and ripped and dirty. No wonder Bigs needed a new one. I felt in the right pocket. Nothing. I felt in the left pocket. I frowned.

I didn't like what I found.

It was a hole. Big enough for a coin to slip through.

I heard Mila's voice outside the door. She was talking extra loudly. It was a warning. "THEY'RE SO CUTE!" she shouted.

I plopped down on the floor and grabbed a Brachiosaurus. Bigs came in, holding a bowl of Gummy Bears. Mila glanced at me. I slid a finger across my nose. It was our secret signal.

Bigs didn't suspect a thing.

Chapter Eight

Rotten

Mila phoned me that night. "You were right," she said. "Lucy says that Bigs was wearing his old green coat when she gave him the coin. She even remembers him putting the coin in his coat pocket." I thanked her and hung up.

I may have been right. But I wished I was wrong. I was already wrong about too many things — mostly Bigs Maloney. The coin probably did fall out of his pocket. It made me feel rotten. It wasn't nice of me to search his room. I was the one who wasn't being honest, not Bigs. He told the truth.

I woke up grumpy Thursday morning. I didn't even talk on the bus with Mila. She called me a grouch and sat with Geetha Nair. At school I saw Bigs Maloney working on his Christmas snowman. He asked if I wanted to help. I didn't feel like it.

For her report, Helen Zuckerman brought in a special candleholder called a menorah. She told us about the eight days of Hanukkah. Her mom made latkes for the whole class. I didn't like tasting new things. It looked like a little pancake, but she couldn't fool me. Helen said they tasted better with applesauce. Oh, brother. Even a cardboard box would taste better with applesauce.

Ms. Gleason got mad at me during reading circle. She said I wasn't acting like a gentleman. She even stopped in the

middle of the story. She said, "Theodore, please stop squirming around like a worm. I'd like you to be sitting on your bottom — and not on your head."

I groaned and sat up straight.

"I'm afraid I might have to send you to the nurse," she said. "I'll tell her, 'This boy sits on his head!'"

The kids laughed. I moped.

"Oh, Theodore," Ms. Gleason said. "You are going to have to do something to turn yourself around today."

Ralphie Jordan shouted out, "Drink some coffee!"

Everybody laughed. Even Mila. Not me.

After lunch, we made snowpeople mobiles to bring home to our parents. It made me feel better. I guess being a mope got boring after a while. So I tried to turn myself around.

To make the snowpeople, we had to measure. We cut three pairs of circles from white construction paper. One pair was two inches in diameter. That means across. One pair was three inches. The last was four inches. I drew a face on the smallest circle. I drew three buttons on the middle circle.

We taped the circles to a long piece of yarn. I used green, because it was a holiday color. Ms. Gleason told us to be careful to leave spaces between the circles. Then we glued on the matching circles. Ms. Gleason

had already cut out a bunch of different hats for us. There were baseball caps, hats with flowers, top hats, and more. I picked a baseball cap and glued it to the head.

Perfect! My mom would love it.

That's when it hit me. *Boing!* My brilliant idea.

See, when Lucy gave Bigs the coin, he was building his Christmas snowman. That's when it probably fell from his pocket. Then I remembered something else. When Mila and I talked to Bigs, I noticed that he wasn't careful. Bigs slapped on handfuls of snow without really looking. He might have picked up the coin by accident.

That's it, I thought. The coin is *inside* Bigs Maloney's snowman!

Chapter Nine

Death of a Snowman

Bigs Maloney hated the idea.

"No way," Bigs said. "I'm not taking him apart. It's going to be my special talent for tomorrow."

"Think about Lucy," Mila said. "She'll be so happy when we find the coin."

Bigs thought that over.

"She might even think you're a hero," I added.

"A hero?" he asked.

"Like Hercules," I said.

Bigs thought some more. Then he stared

at his snowman for a long time. "Okay," he agreed. "I'll do it."

The three of us met at the snowman after school. Little by little, we chipped off pieces. We carefully searched through the snow. After a while, it was a headless snowman. Then we took apart the middle. Finally there was no more snowman left. We found pebbles. We found small sticks. But we didn't find the coin. So much for my brilliant idea. We were tired and unhappy.

It was getting dark. Mila patted Bigs Maloney's shoulder. "Cheer up, Bigs. At least we tried."

Bigs looked at Mila. He looked at me. Then he hung his head, sighed, and slowly walked home.

He didn't even say good-bye.

I lay in bed that night — thinking and thinking and thinking. I sat up and turned on the light. I took out my detective journal. Inside, pressed neatly between the pages, was a five-dollar bill. I laid it on my night table. If I didn't solve this case soon, I'd have to return the money to Lucy Hiller.

But I didn't become the best detective in second grade by giving up so easily. Every mystery had a solution. I just needed to find the right clue.

My mom says that when you think too hard, it only makes things worse. So I tried *not* to think. It's pretty much impossible. I tried not thinking about a lot of different things. I tried not to think about Bigs or Lucy or the snowman or the missing coin. In the end, I tried not to think about my vocabulary words: *shoe, shut, large, find, sweep. . . .*

I sat up in bed. That's it! I thought. The solution was right there all the time — in my homework!

Chapter Ten

One Last Hope

On the bus Friday morning, I handed my old homework sheet to Mila. "Look," I said. "Here's the missing clue."

Mila shook her head. "I don't get it, Jigsaw. This is your homework."

"There," I said, pointing to the word *sweep*. "Look at the sentence I wrote."

I like to SWEEP.

Mila made a face. "So?"

"Now look at the sentence I wrote for the word *find.*"

I like to FIND clues.

Mila crossed her arms. She rocked back and forth. It was how she got her thinking machine started. "Sorry, Jigsaw. I *still* don't get it."

"Let me connect the dots for you," I said. "The other day, I did a math problem about a school janitor. That got me thinking about Mr. Copabianco and how he's always finding stuff."

Mila nodded. I continued, "Then I thought about our spelling homework. *Sweep. Find.*"

Mila's face brightened. "You don't think . . . ?"

"That's exactly what I think," I said. "Maybe — just maybe — Bigs dropped the coin inside the school."

“And maybe,” Mila added, “Good Old Mr. Copabianco found it when he swept the floors!”

We raced to room 201. Ms. Gleason was standing in the doorway. That wasn’t a great spot for her to stand. We almost knocked her over.

“Slow down, you two,” she said. “This isn’t the Indy 500.”

“Oops, sorry!” I said. “We have to talk to Mr. Copabianco. It’s a super emergency.”

“An emergency? What happened now? Is the toilet in the boys’ room overflowing again?” Ms. Gleason asked.

“Worse,” I whispered. “But we can’t tell you here. It’s private.”

Ms. Gleason stood up and flicked the lights on and off. “Boys and girls, I’m going to count to five. I want you all to find a seat. One, two, three, four, five.” Everyone sat down. Ms. Gleason smiled. “Great job. Please read silently. I’ll be right outside the door.”

In the hallway, Ms. Gleason stood in front of us. “Tell me all about it.”

So we told her about the missing nickel. And about Bigs Maloney. And the hole in his pocket. And the ruined Christmas snowman. “Mr. Copabianco is our last hope,” I said.

Ms. Gleason took a deep breath. That was a good sign. She always sighed before saying yes. When we left, she said, “Don’t take too long. It wouldn't be a class party without you."

Mila and I raced down the hallway. We were hoping as hard as we could hope. We crossed all of our fingers, even thumbs. We heard Good Old Mr. Copabianco whistling in the janitor's room. It was "Jingle Bells." We knocked.

"Come on in," he shouted. "Nobody's in here but us chickens!"

"Mr. Copabianco," I said slowly. "Did

you — by any chance — find a nickel on school property?"

He opened a drawer and placed a heavy glass jar on the table. "I find change nearly every day," he said, "mostly in the cafeteria. I just toss it into this jar at the end of the day." He pointed to a box. "Plus I find toys, scarves, mittens, tennis balls — you name it. I keep it all right here."

I barely listened. I was too busy staring at the glass jar. It was filled with coins. Mr.

Copabianco said, "I save up all the change I find. At the end of the year, I donate it to Save the Children. I figure the money isn't really mine. At least this way, it does some good in the world."

He tilted his head toward the jar. "Go ahead, kids. If you lost a nickel, you're free to take one." We told him that it wasn't just any nickel. It was a 1937D Indian head, with a three-legged buffalo.

You could have knocked him down with a feather.

He spilled the jar on the table. "Let's dig in, kids. A coin like that is worth hundreds."

Chapter Eleven

The Amazing Jones

Mila was the one who found it. That's because she has good eyes. Mr. Copabianco held the coin under his desk lamp. He whistled softly. "It's a little scratched," he said. "But I'd say it was in excellent condition." He handed the coin to me. "I guess this is yours."

Don't ask *why* I did what I did next.

I reached into my pocket. I pulled out the five-dollar bill. I looked at the jar. I looked at Mila. Somehow, she knew what I was thinking. Mila nodded. "It's okay, Jigsaw," she said. "It's Christmas. It's a time for giving."

So I stuffed Abraham Lincoln into the jar.

Trumpets didn't sound. Bluebirds didn't sing. Angels didn't call my name. Nothing changed at all. Nothing, I guess, except I was five dollars lighter.

But I felt good inside. Like I had done something right.

We got back to room 201 just in time to

see Joey Pignattano smash his pinkie. It was part of the talent show. Joey was doing his Tae Kwon Do demonstration. He was dressed in a white uniform. He called it a tunic. I would have called it white pajamas with a belt. But never mind.

Joey started by doing all sorts of crazy kicks and spinning something-or-others. Then he did a bunch of I-don't-know-whatcha-ma-call-its. Anyway, he punched the air a lot. But one time, I guess he got too close to Ms. Gleason's desk. *Whack!* He smacked his pinkie pretty good. Joey didn't cry or anything, but you could tell it hurt.

Everybody clapped anyway.

After things settled down, Ms. Gleason came over to us. "Any luck?" she whispered.

I smiled and slid a finger across my nose. It was a secret signal. But Ms. Gleason seemed to understand. "Can I take a turn?" I asked.

I walked in front of the room. "Welcome, ladies and gentlemen," I said in a loud voice. "My name is the Amazing Jones. I will now amaze you with a trick." I really hammed it up. "Without speaking a word, I will make Lucy Hiller jump up and down and scream."

Lucy gave me a look. I winked.

"Lucy, could you come up here, please?"

Lucy walked up beside me. "What's going on?" she whispered.

I didn't answer. I rolled up my sleeves. I held out my hands. Then I reached into my pocket — and placed something in Lucy's palm. She looked. It was the missing 1937D Indian-head nickel.

Sure enough, Lucy jumped up and down. She screamed. She danced. She hugged me and Mila and Bigs Maloney.

I guess I had a special talent after all.

Then we got to open our grab bag treats. After that, I noticed Ms. Gleason talking with Bigs Maloney. They were whispering. At first Bigs looked a little sad. Then Ms. Gleason looked up at the clock. She talked some more. I watched Bigs Maloney's frown turn upside down. He was smiling.

Ms. Gleason flicked the lights to get our attention. She told us her great idea. Everyone cheered. In a flash, we were all lined up and dressed in our winter coats.

"Isn't this fun?" Ms. Gleason said. "What

a wonderful way to finish the last day of class before vacation."

Everybody spilled onto the playground. We sang Christmas songs as we ran. Everybody was laughing and hooting and acting silly.

Smack! A snowball hit me. Right in the back.

"Bull's-eye!" I heard Bigs scream.

I looked at him and smiled. I didn't mind. What can you do? When Bigs Maloney saw

snow, he just had to make a snowball. And if he had a snowball, well, he had to throw it. I guess it wasn't his fault that I made a perfect target.

"Let's get started, boys and girls," Ms. Gleason shouted. "This is going to be the biggest Christmas snowman ever!"

And it was. Even Bigs thought so.

"Nice snowman," I said to Bigs.

"Yeah," he said. "It's pretty good." Bigs looked away. "Thanks," he mumbled.

I put out my hand. "Friends?" I said.
"Friends," Bigs said.
Then he did something I never expected.
The big lug hugged me.
Yeesh.